KT-479-166

play forever on video and Disney DVD

© Disney

Published by Ladybird Books Ltd.
A Penguin Company
Penguin Books Ltd., 80 Strand, London WC2R 0RL
Penguin Books Australia Ltd., Camberwell, Victoria, Australia
Penguin Books (NZ) Ltd., Private Bag 102902, NSMC, Auckland,
New Zealand

WALT DISNEY'S

CLASSIC

DUMBO

Ladybird

It was morning at the circus. Hopeful mothers looked up as storks flew overhead. Each stork carried a tiny bundle which held a baby animal. When the storks dropped the bundles, parachutes opened and the baby animals floated down to the ground.

Mrs Jumbo sighed as she watched the happy mothers cuddling their babies. "Oh, dear. I did so hope there would be a bundle for me," she said.

Mrs Jumbo sadly joined the other animals waiting to be loaded onto the circus train.

That day, the circus was moving on to another town. As the train chuffed along, a voice called, "Mrs Jumbo!" It was a stork struggling to carry a *very* heavy bundle.

Mrs Jumbo shared a carriage with four other elephants. They waved their trunks and called, "Yoo, hoo! Mr Stork, over here!"

The stork flew into the carriage and dropped the large bundle beside Mrs Jumbo. She opened it eagerly. Inside was a baby elephant – Jumbo Junior.

"Look at him!" cried the other elephants, excitedly. "Isn't he *adorable*!"

Just then, Mrs Jumbo's baby sneezed.
Out flapped two *enormous* ears!

The other elephants gasped. Then
they began to giggle. They thought
baby Jumbo looked so funny that he
ought to be called – Dumbo!

Mrs Jumbo didn't care what the other
elephants thought. She loved her
baby no matter what he looked like.
She lifted him up in her trunk and
gently rocked him to sleep.

That night, the circus train stopped
and all the animals climbed out.
The circus men put up a huge tent.

Next morning, the circus parade
made its way through the town.
People clapped and cheered. The
band played and the clowns and
animals marched down the street.

Crowds hurried to the circus tent that night. They were eager to see all the animals. A group of noisy boys gathered round the elephants.

"Look at his ears!" cried one, pointing at Dumbo. "Aren't they the funniest things you ever saw?"

The boys laughed and teased Dumbo. Then one of them pulled the little elephant's ears.

Mrs Jumbo trumpeted with anger.
She grabbed the naughty boy and
smacked him with her trunk.

Everyone thought Mrs Jumbo had gone mad. They screamed and tried to get away. The Ringmaster came rushing over to help.

"Down! Down!" he cried, cracking his whip. But Mrs Jumbo just became more and more angry.

Soon, Dumbo's mother was tied up
and taken away. She was locked in a
small cage far away from Dumbo
and the other animals.

Back in the tent, the other elephants gossiped about Dumbo's mother.

"Such disgraceful behaviour!" they said. "It's all *his* fault, you know." And they turned and glared at Dumbo.

Nearby, a mouse called Timothy was watching. He felt sorry for the little elephant.

"I'll be your friend," Timothy told Dumbo. "In fact, I'll bet we can make you famous. All we need is a good plan…"

Just then, they heard the Ringmaster
talking in his tent. "I've got an idea!"
he was saying. "We will make an
enormous pyramid of elephants! All
it needs is a *big* finish!"

So, as soon as the Ringmaster was asleep, Timothy crept into his tent. He scampered up to the Ringmaster's ear and said, "Your big finish is the little elephant with the big ears – Dumbo!"

"Dumbo…" mumbled the Ringmaster. "Dumbo…"

Next morning, the Ringmaster tried out his new idea…

In the centre of the circus ring the elephants balanced carefully on top of one another. They waited for Dumbo to jump to the very top of the pyramid of elephants.

But as Dumbo ran, he tripped over his ears and bumped into the pyramid. The elephants crashed to the ground and the whole tent fell down around them.

Now the elephants were angrier than ever with Dumbo. But the Ringmaster had another idea – Dumbo could become a clown!

So Dumbo was dressed like a baby and put at the very top of a burning building. The other clowns pretended to be firefighters. They sprayed Dumbo with water and held a hoop for him to jump into.

Poor Dumbo was terrified as he jumped.

Down and down he dropped until he fell through the hoop into a tub of sticky gunge! The audience cheered and roared with laughter.

The clowns were pleased with the success of their act. After the show they drank champagne to celebrate.

But poor Dumbo wasn't invited to the celebrations. He sat outside the clowns' tent, crying softly. Timothy gently washed the gunge from the little elephant's head.

Then, Timothy thought of a way to cheer up his friend. "We'll go and see your mother!" he said.

Dumbo and his mother were
overjoyed to see each other again.
Mrs Jumbo put her trunk through the
bars of her cage and cuddled her son.

   "You are so precious to me,
      Cute as can be,
      Baby of mine,"
she sang, holding him tenderly.

But all too soon it was time for Dumbo
to go. He didn't want to leave his
mother. After they had said goodbye,
he cried so hard that he got hiccups.

"Here, have a drink," said Timothy, leading Dumbo to a water bucket in the clowns' tent.

As Dumbo and Timothy drank, they began to feel strange. They didn't realise that a bottle of champagne had emptied into the bucket!

Before long, Dumbo and Timothy
felt *very* strange indeed! And they
began seeing strange things too – a
whole parade of pink elephants
seemed to march past them!

The next thing Dumbo and Timothy
knew it was morning. When they
opened their eyes, they saw a gang
of crows looking at them.

Dumbo and Timothy were high up
on the branch of a tree!

The little elephant was so surprised that he lost his balance. He tried to grab hold of the branch with his trunk, but it snapped. Dumbo and Timothy tumbled through the air until they landed in a pond far below.

"I wonder how we got in that tree," said Timothy, shaking himself dry.

"Maybe you flew!" joked one of the crows.

"Yes, that's it!" cried Timothy. "Dumbo, you *flew* up there!" The little elephant looked surprised. He couldn't really fly – could he?

Timothy and the crows guessed that
Dumbo *could* fly – the little elephant
just had to believe it himself!

One crow gave Timothy an ordinary
feather and whispered, "This is a
magic feather. It will help Dumbo fly!"

Holding the feather in his trunk,
Dumbo stood at the edge of a cliff.
Before he could change his mind, the
crows pushed him. All at once,
Dumbo was flapping through the air.

That night at the circus, Dumbo
stood at the top of the burning
building. He didn't feel frightened.
Now that he had the magic feather
he knew he could fly down safely.

Timothy was tucked inside Dumbo's hat. "Okay," he said. "Take off!"

Just as the little elephant leapt into the air he dropped the feather!

As Dumbo began to fall, Timothy cried, "Flap your ears! You *can* fly! You can!"

Dumbo took a deep breath and began to flap his ears as fast as he could. Suddenly, Dumbo was flying!

The Ringmaster was amazed! He watched Dumbo swoop over the tub of gunge and soar past the cheering crowds. Dumbo was a star!

Before long, Dumbo was famous all around the world. Crowds flocked to the circus to see "Dumbo, the Amazing Flying Elephant".

The Ringmaster was so pleased that
he ordered the release of Dumbo's
mother. In fact, he gave Mrs Jumbo a
special railway carriage of her own.

Timothy's promise had come true –
Dumbo, the little flying elephant,
had become famous. But best of all,
everybody loved him!

Yours
to own
on ∂ISNEY
DVD

Magical stories to